Blackberry Juice

Blackberry Juice

Sara Cassidy

Illustrated by Helen Flook

ORCA BOOK PUBLISHERS

Library and Archives Canada Cataloguing in Publication

Cassidy, Sara, author
Blackberry juice / Sara Cassidy ; illustrated by Helen Flook.
(Orca echoes)

Issued in print and electronic formats.
ISBN 978-1-4598-1228-4 (paperback).—ISBN 978-1-4598-1229-1 (pdf).—
ISBN 978-1-4598-1230-7 (epub)

I. Flook, Helen, illustrator II. Title. III. Series: Orca echoes
PS8555.A7812B53 2016   jc813'.54   C2016-900465-1
C2016-900466-X

First published in the United States, 2016
Library of Congress Control Number: 2016931874

Summary: In this early chapter book and follow up to *Not For Sale*, Cyrus and his brother, Rudy,
adjust to life in the country after moving into their new house.

Orca Book Publishers gratefully acknowledges the support for its publishing programs
provided by the following agencies: the Government of Canada through the Canada Book Fund
and the Canada Council for the Arts, and the Province of British Columbia
through the BC Arts Council and the Book Publishing Tax Credit.

Cover artwork and interior illustrations by Helen Flook
Author photo by Amaya Tarasoff

ORCA BOOK PUBLISHERS
www.orcabook.com

Printed and bound in Canada.

19 18 17 16 • 4 3 2 1

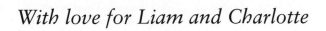

With love for Liam and Charlotte

Chapter One

Where are the sudsy sheep and the horses with velvet noses? The grumbling tractors and shiny silos? When Mom said we were moving to a farmhouse, I pictured a wide front porch and a tire swing strung from a huge tree.

Like in a picture book. But I guess real life isn't a picture book.

We've unfolded our bodies from the stinky moving van. Rudy, my little brother, holds the mason jar with our goldfish, Einstein. I hold Wigglechin, our cat, whose fur is standing on end. We're staring at a crooked, porchless house in a ragged yard, beside a gap-toothed barn with a slumped roof.

"So it needs a little love," Dad says. He ruffles Rudy's hair and kisses Mom on the cheek. "Too bad I've got to go."

He tosses me into a mangy haystack, then untangles his bike from a lamp in the back of the van. He slings an enormous duffel bag over his shoulder as if it's as light as a cloud, then pedals down the gravel road, getting smaller and smaller until he's the size of a fly. Then—*poof*—he disappears.

Dad is headed to the airport to
catch a bush plane. Dad's a lumberjack.
He operates a feller buncher, which
fells trees, then *bunches* them into piles.

He's gone half the time, living in logging camps, but I'm used to missing him.

Mom reaches into her jeans pocket and drops a couple of coins in my hand. "Okay, Cyrus, go to the neighbors' and get us some eggs."

"You want me to go to a strange house and ask for their eggs?"

"They keep hens, silly." Mom points to a painted square of wood nailed to a tree.

"They spell funny," I say.

"The world is filled with all kinds of folks," Mom says. "And that's a good thing."

Rudy scrambles up a tree. He's eight. I'm nine. Scrambling up high is what Rudy does when he's anxious. He squats on countertops or sits cross-legged on the piano or even on top of the fridge. Today, he might be anxious because we've left the only home we've ever known. Or maybe because our new house looks like it's about to collapse. Or maybe he just doesn't want Mom to ask *him* to get eggs.

A narrow driveway winds up to the neighbors' house. "It's so far," I whine.

"That's the country for you," Mom says. "It's a long way between neighbors."

"Is *that* a good thing?"

"It can be."

I point to the blocky white shapes in the neighbors' field. "Are those bulls? Because I'm not going if—"

Mom clears her throat.

"Okay, I'm going." I shake my finger at the tree. "Don't go exploring until I'm back."

"I'll be here," Rudy promises, his voice muffled by the wide summer leaves.

Halfway up the neighbors' mile-long driveway, I trip on a pothole and hit the ground in a cloud of dust. The blocky shapes trot over. I hurry to my feet and brush myself off. I offer the cows handfuls of grass, but they turn up their noses, which are like dog noses, only more slobbery. Every so often a huge tongue comes out and goes right up a nostril. If people could do that, there'd be a law against it.

Closer to the house, I'm mobbed by a clucking crowd of chickens. They peck at my shoes and shins and follow me up the stairs to the sagging porch. On top of a small, dirty fridge is a dented cookie tin labeled *Munny*. Five egg cartons huddle inside the fridge, the eggs so big the cartons have to be held shut with thick rubber bands. I drop the coins into the tin. *Clink-clink.* The feathered mob is now tugging on my shoelaces.

Someone swings down to the porch from—where? The roof? The sky? "They think your shoelaces are worms," the girl says. She's wearing all orange—orange T-shirt, orange pants, orange socks, orange shoes. Her thick black braid is tied up with an orange elastic. Her fingernails are painted orange.

"I'm guessing you're a fan of the color between red and yellow," I say.

"What do you mean?"

"Your, um, attire."

"I am not a tire."

"I mean, your outfit. By the way, *eggs* is spelled with two *g*'s."

The girl scowls at me. "I made the sign when I was four." She looks at the carton in my hand. "Most people drive up for their eggs."

"I'm too young to drive. Plus I live super close. Next door, in fact."

"Since when?"

"Five minutes ago. Maybe six— your driveway is very long."

I squat and sort out my hen-pecked laces.

"What's your name?" the girl asks.

"Cyrus."

"Well, Cy," the girl says, shimmying up a post, "enjoy the eggs-with-two-*g*'s."

No one ever calls me Cy. Rudy's the one with the nickname. Of course, no one's allowed to say his full name, which is a great name if you're a reindeer. Dad says there was a famous artist named Cy Twombly. I looked him up once. His work was like scribbling, which didn't surprise me since his last name sounds like a scribble. A scribble crossed with a mumble.

"Hey!" I yell when I'm halfway down the driveway. The girl is hauling herself over a railing onto a third-floor porch. Mom would make me wear a helmet if I wanted to do that. And elbow pads and knee pads. And hockey pants and shin guards. And my mouth guard. Plus a seat belt. "What's *your* name?"

"Pardon?"

"*What's your name?*" I shout.

The girl cups a hand behind her ear. "I can't hear you."

"WHAT IS YOUR NAME??" I yell. I practically break my throat.

"Rachel." The girl laughs. "I heard you the first time."

Chapter Two

Mom's on the phone, which is connected to the kitchen wall with a curly cord like a pig's tail. She seems upset.

"I didn't know it came with the house. Yes, I read the fine print. Okay, not *all* the fine print. The magnifying glass was broken. Well, at least tell me how to feed it."

Rudy hops onto the counter. "Feed *what*?"

Mom points to the back door. "Feast your eyes, boys."

I beat Rudy to the door. I yank it open and can't believe what I'm seeing. A large swaybacked, sad-looking, fuzzy-eared animal is nibbling on a patch of the overgrown lawn.

An anxious hand tightens around my ankle. "That's not a horse," Rudy says.

I loosen his fingers so that my leg can breathe. "You're right, brother."

Rudy and I approach the beast. Its tail stops moving. I stroke its back. Its ears point forward. I think it's nervous. Even scared.

I've always liked donkeys. I like how they bray—part laugh, part sob, part sneeze. This one is all gray except for a white nose and a white line across

its shoulders and another down its back. But the animal's thin, and its fur is missing in spots.

"It's not very lively," Rudy says.

"It's old, I think. Maybe sad too."

"Why?"

"I don't know, Rudy," I snap.

Rudy's eyes fill with tears. "Are you sad?"

"About what?"

"About leaving the cherry tree and the tinkly dining-room chandelier and the bathroom with two doors—"

Rudy's earlobes turn red. He's about to cry.

"I'm not sad," I say. "I'm angry. It's stupid that we had to leave the city."

We stand in the backyard for ages, Rudy sobbing a little while I stroke the donkey's neck. After a while Mom appears at the back door. "Well," she says. "You've always wanted a dog."

I find porridge oats in a box labeled *Kitchen Stuff*. I wave them under the donkey's muzzle until finally he snuffles them up from the palm of my hand. His muzzle isn't as slobbery as the cows'. It's not as velvety as a horse's either.

We hardly ever call Dad at camp because the phone connection is so bad. But we can't wait to tell him the strange news.

"A wrong key?" he asks.

"No, a donkey!"

"A door key?"

"A *donkey*."

"A doggie?"

"A DONKEY!"

"I keep thinking you're saying *donkey*."

"We *are* saying *donkey*!"

Chapter Three

"What is with these egg yolks?" I reach for Mom's sunglasses. "They're blinding me. They're brighter than dog pee in fresh snow."

"*Cyrus!*"

"He's right," Rudy agrees. "They're dynamic. Blazing. Fervid."

"Fervid?"

Rudy holds up a book with a tattered cover and its pages trying to escape.

"Found it in the attic. It's a thesaurus. A dictionary that lists words that mean the same thing. It's interesting. Fascinating. Compelling."

"You should have seen the eggs before Mom cracked them. They were all muddy, with straw and feathers stuck to the shells."

"I don't think that was mud," Mom says. She raises an eyebrow.

"That's disgusting," I say. "We left the city to eat disgusting, dirty eggs?"

"Listen. The yolks are bright because instead of living in boring factories, eating boring food, the chickens run around in the fresh air, eating colorful plants. That makes their yolks happy. And now, instead of living in a boring city with polluted air, you live in the country with loads of fresh air. That will make your hearts happy."

"My heart *was* happy," I say. "All of me was." I'm following the swirls on the tablecloth with my fingertip. One swirl leads to another. I could trace the whole cloth without lifting my finger. I've been trying to since I was little, but something always interrupts me, or I get bored. "Mom, you called this place a *farm*house, but where's the farm?"

"It used to be a farm. But it was too close to the ocean. There was too much salt in the ground for stuff to grow. You've seen the barn."

"Some barn. The roof is caving in, and the whole place is splattered with pigeon poo."

"Guano," Rudy says, flipping through his book. "Droppings, scat, manure…"

There's a knock at the front door. "Answer it, Cyrus," Mom says, running into the bedroom.

I swing open the wide door. Standing on the step is *eg* girl with an old man. The girl is all in purple today—purple T-shirt, purple shorts, purple sandals. Even the Band-Aid on her knee is purple. I glance at her fingernails, but she draws her hands into fists. I look down, but she quickly curls her toes under.

"Did you know there's no full rhyme for *purple*?" I ask.

Rachel glares.

"*Gerbil* comes close," the old man says. "And *burble*. But heck, a whole lot of English words have no rhyme. *Sausage, steamroller, bulb, angel, silver, month, welcome.*" He holds out a pie with a

crisscross top. "Speaking of welcome, here's a pie. Blackberry. To welcome you to the neighborhood."

Mom crashes into the entrance way. "How wonderful!" Her T-shirt is inside out, and her hair is a static ball. She has changed out of her pajamas in record time.

"The name's Jedediah," the old man says, shaking Mom's hand. "Everyone calls me Jerry though. My wife, Cornelia—people call her Corny—was sorry she couldn't come. She's been under the weather. This is Rachel, our granddaughter, who moved in with us last fall."

Mom eyes the pie. "That looks lovely."

"It's never too early for a slice," Jerry says, winking.

A second later, we're at the breakfast table. While Rachel is focused on getting every last crumb onto her fork, I sneak a look at her fingernails, which are, as I suspected, painted to match her outfit. They also match the pie. Her tongue does too. I stick out my tongue to see if it's also dyed with berry juice. I can't quite tell.

"This is really good pie," Mom says.

"We picked the berries yesterday," Jerry says. "Basically, they're still alive."

A berry falls off my fork and onto the tablecloth. I cover the splash with my napkin before Mom sees. She is telling Jerry about the donkey that magically appeared in the backyard.

"His name is Rumpley," Jerry says. "He belonged to my brother, Hector, who lived in this house for forty years. He kept Rumpley out front though. He would sit and talk with him there for hours. Sometimes it was like they were having a conversation, with Rumpley nickering and braying while Hector yammered on."

Rudy flips through his ancient book. "Nicker. Whinny. Neigh."

"Blow, snort, groan, grunt, sigh," Jerry says. "Donkeys make all sorts of noises. And each noise means something different. Dear Hector knew the language. He died two years ago. The city couple that bought the house hid Rumpley away in the back."

"More pie?" Mom asks.

"Don't mind if I do." Jerry holds out his plate. "It's a very fine pie. You'll have to give me your recipe."

Chapter Four

"I can guess why the donkey's name is Rumpley." Rudy is squatting in front of the old thesaurus. "I looked up his name, but it wasn't in the thesaurus. There was only *rump*. Which, you know, means, well, bum. I looked up *donkey*, and there's a word, a bit of a swearword."

"You're supposed to be helping me," I grumble. I'm pulling Rumpley around to the front yard to the exact spot where he used to stand. Jerry showed me. Rumpley moves slowly, but he's getting livelier, I think. For three weeks I've been brushing him every day and giving him fresh water and barley straw. I researched all about donkeys online, but Wi-Fi isn't good in the country—it sputters on and off. You get the best reception in the bathroom, standing on the toilet.

There's something sad about Rumpley that I just want to cheer up. When I finally get him into his old spot, he takes a slow look around. He stares for a while at Wigglechin, our cat, who is hanging from the vines that cover the crooked farmhouse. Wigglechin is often clinging to things she's trying not to fall from. In our old house, you'd find her

clutching the living-room curtains or the dining-room chandelier. Here, she swings from tree branches, fences, even the barn door. I think she likes being outside. One thing about the country: there's lots of outside.

"Remember your old spot?" I whisper into Rumpley's soft ear. I hope that maybe he'll whinny and nod his head, but he doesn't.

Rudy grabs my elbow and squeezes. Something is rustling in the bushes. But it isn't a wild animal or a band of thieves. It's Rachel. She steps out, dressed all in green. Green sandals, green shorts, green shirt, green bow on her braid, green necklace. I check her fingernails. She doesn't curl them out of sight. Green.

"You must have a lot of layers—" I say.

"Nine," she says. "There's a chip here on my thumbnail where you can count the last five."

"Like a Gobstopper."

"Exactly."

"Why didn't you tell me about that shortcut?"

"You never asked."

Rachel nods toward Rumpley, who's munching on the long grass at his feet. "He looks happier."

"Do you think so?" My heart lifts.

"I do. If you ever want to braid ribbons into his mane, let me know."

Rachel points to a flower bed filled with velvety flowers. "That's the exact spot where Great-Uncle Hector died."

Rudy springs up a tree.

"He had a massive heart attack. He was gone"—Rachel snaps her fingers—

"like *that*. Grandpa planted the pansies to mark the spot. He misses his brother. After two years, he still keeps the flag at half-mast." Rachel squints at the flag in her front yard. "Holy! Is that your cat?"

Wigglechin has climbed the flagpole and is now twirling and flailing, her claws sunk into the silky fabric. I can't tell if she's having fun or is terrified.

Rudy runs for Jerry while Rachel and I yank a bedsheet from the clothesline and stretch it between us to catch Wigglechin if she falls.

"Do you like living here?" I ask as we stand duty at the bottom of the flagpole. The blocky white cows are gathering around us, their giant tongues zooming in and out of their giant nostrils.

"I've gotten the hang of it."

"Where are your parents anyway?"

Rachel's face hardens.

"Sorry," I say. "It's none of my business, right?"

"Mom visits every Sunday. She's trying to get a good job and an apartment, but it's hard for her. She went back to school, too, and that's expensive and it takes up all her time. She was really young when I was born."

"So your grandparents are like your parents."

"For now, yeah. They're nice. Grandpa gets silly, but Grandma's serious. It balances out."

"I was adopted too," I blurt. "Ages ago. When I was a baby. So you and I are sort of alike."

Rachel smiles.

"And we both have a diastema," I say.

"Diastema?"

"This space." I stick my tongue through the gap between my front teeth.

Rachel pushes her tongue against her gap and blows. She whistles a high-pitched *whheeet*.

"I wish I could do that."

"I'll teach you." Wigglechin scrabbles and yowls above us. She loses her grip and ends up hanging by one paw. "When we're done here," Rachel adds.

Rudy and Jerry come hurrying across the field. Jerry is holding a giant tin of sardines in one hand and a can opener in the other. "For when the cat comes down. To lessen the shock."

"Like how you gave me ice cream when I got the bee sting," Rachel says.

"That's right. To take the sting out. Soften the blow." Jerry winks at me.

"Making friends in new places can do that too."

Jerry starts lowering the flag, hand over hand on the rope. Wigglechin's ears go up when she feels herself jerking downward. She starts wriggling.

Rrr-i-ppp! The flag tears in two, and Wigglechin plummets, yowling. Rachel and I are in the right place. We catch her!

Jerry opens the sardines, and before you know it, Wigglechin steps out of the sheet and starts munching on a row of shiny fish as if nothing ever happened.

"Sorry about the flag," I tell Jerry, gathering up the pieces.

"As long as no one's hurt. Besides, Corny has a gift for mending."

Jerry puts his arm around Rachel and gives her a squeeze, his smile

showing off his own diastema. His arm on Rachel's shoulders is like a stitch, threading them close.

I crouch down and stroke Wigglechin's gray fur.

Clatter-clatter. Wigglechin drags the sardine tin under a hedge to eat in privacy.

Chapter Five

I spend time every day feeding and brushing and talking to Rumpley. I think he lost his confidence at some point. I'm building it back up by telling him about who he is.

"You're a member of the Equidae family, a cousin of horses and zebras," I repeat from Wikipedia. "Donkeys have helped build the world. You've hauled silver, gold, grain and lumber. You're calm, loyal workers."

I don't mention that the donkey has been called "the poor man's horse," or that the Romans thought it was bad luck to meet a donkey. Or that donkeys are often considered ignorant and foolish.

Instead, I tell him the Iranian legend about the enormous three-legged donkey with nine mouths and six eyes that stands in the middle of the ocean and cleans the world's water. I tell him how a Hindu donkey pulls the chariot of the Divine Twins, the great gods of good and evil, and that donkey manure is the best fertilizer if you want to grow pomegranates.

Today, for the first time, Rumpley whinnies when I approach with his daily apple, and he leans toward me when I brush him. Until now he has just stood there, as if asleep. But today the warm weight of him tips in my favor.

I wonder if he will ever bray.

Jerry says he hasn't brayed since Hector died.

After lunch Mom plunks a large potato in Rudy's hand and one in mine. "You kids have been helping a lot around here," she says. "Go have some fun."

We grab our potato guns and head to the beach, where Rudy wades into the water, then runs back toward me, splashing and screaming garble. It's the start of World War II. Our little inlet is Pearl Harbor, and Japan is attacking the Americans. I hide behind a boulder and shoot a few potato pellets his way.

Suddenly my feet are frozen, and cold creeps up my pant legs. I'm standing in a tidal pool. Great!

A tidal pool is a bowl of seawater that stays behind in the dips and hollows of beach rocks when the tide goes out. At first, tidal pools look like boring puddles, but if you stare for a while, a wet kingdom unfolds. With anemones, water beetles, snails, barnacles, seaweeds, limpets and little fish, all busy surviving.

At my feet a crab is trying to get out from under a rock. The problem is,

I'm standing on the rock! I lift my foot and the crab gets free—but its leg is broken, bent the wrong way. The crab drags it behind her as she moves away.

That's one thing about the country—animals are always getting hurt. Or worse. I've found worms that Rachel has biked over—her tire tread imprinted across their bellies—and banana slugs smushed by people who weren't watching where they were going.

Wigglechin was coming home with hummingbirds in her jaw until we put a bell on her collar.

Dead flies hang over our breakfast table, stuck to a strip of syrupy paper. It's awful.

Maybe I should snap the crab's leg off. Or make it some kind of cast.

A shadow darkens the tidal pool. Rudy has snuck up and is pointing his potato gun at my knee. We aren't allowed to aim higher. "Drop your weapon. You're a prisoner of war."

"Look what I did to the crab," I say with a moan.

"You're still my prisoner of war."

"I broke its leg!"

"Why?"

"Not on purpose!"

"Should we call a vet?"

"I don't think there's a doctor for crabs."

"We have to help it," Rudy says.

"We'll take it home."

"It could live in the aquarium."

I get an ugly picture in my mind of the crab waving Einstein about in its pincers. "The bathtub would be better," I suggest.

I pick up the crab the way Dad taught me—thumb under her big orange shell, index finger on top. All other fingers out of the way. I check the markings on her underbelly. They sketch a lighthouse rather than a pyramid, which means she's female.

"Let's call her Helen," I say, remembering the super nice librarian at our old school. Helen is a warm name, a soft blanket for this cold, crunchy creature. A name is like a shelter, I realize, something you live in. A home you never move out of.

Chapter Six

Rudy and I put Helen into the bathtub with an inch of water. We build a Lego platform for her to climb or to hide under, then head up to the attic to play Settlers of Catan. The attic is boiling hot and smells like a lot of bad breath, and the carpet is rough on our knees, but for some reason we like hanging out up here. We're on to a second game of Settlers of Catan when Mom calls up,

"Boys? When were you going to tell me about the crab?"

"Helen," I yell down.

"What?"

"Her name is Helen," Rudy explains.

"Okay, then, when were you going to tell me about *Helen*?" Mom climbs the creaky stairs.

"Helen just needs to be somewhere safe right now," I say.

"So her leg can heal," Rudy adds.

"The safest place for a crab is the sea," Mom says. "There's everything that it, uh, that *Helen* needs. Seaweed, for one. And salt water."

"We added salt," Rudy says.

Mom bites her lip. "She needs rocks to hide under, and sunshine, and the tide coming and going. That's her home. You took her out of her home."

"Well, you took us out of our home," I say.

"Yeah," Rudy chimes in. Then he clamps his hand over his mouth and springs up onto a dresser. Rudy hates confrontation.

"Look," Mom says. "Life is as good here as it was in the city."

"It is not," I say. "The eggs are dirty, and dust pours in the windows whenever someone drives by, and dead flies swing over our heads while we eat breakfast."

Mom is not moved. "Return. The. Crab."

"Helen," Rudy reminds her.

Mom is taking Rudy to the city to get a haircut from Burt the barber, since Dad's coming home tomorrow. I got a haircut last week. A surprise one. I was climbing the pine tree behind the barn and a glop of sap basically leapt on me. Google suggested washing it out with peanut butter, but I got the scissors instead.

Before Mom and Rudy head out, she puts her hands on my shoulders, squats down and looks me in the eye. "There will be no crabs in the house when I get back."

I look at my feet. They're bare and dirty. I wiggle my toes. I hardly ever saw my feet in the city. "Okay."

As soon as Mom and Rudy are gone, I kneel on the shaggy oval carpet beside the tub. There's a matching carpet that fits snugly around the base of the toilet. And a matching toilet seat cover too. The fuzzy, pink constellation came with the house. Mom says she has a love-hate relationship with it.

Uh-oh.

Helen is at one end of the tub, under the Lego platform.

Her leg is at the other end.

"Oh, Helen. I'm sorry." I get a thumb under her belly. "I still have to take you home."

I step into my rubber boots and head outside. It's late afternoon, and the air is cool. Wigglechin is hanging off the neighbors' fence. Rumpley is snuffling at the flowers Jerry planted for his brother. "See you later," I say, stroking Rumpley's warm neck with my one free hand. He doesn't look up. At least his ears are back. That's a sign he feels calm. Maybe Rachel was right—maybe Rumpley *is* happier these days. "You're the best," I whisper in his fuzzy ear.

The tide has come in, which means Helen's original tidal pool is underwater. I'll have to find another one. I climb onto a rock where water is caught in a crevice, but it isn't enough. There's no life in it, not even barnacles. I jump to another large rock. This one has a *huge* tidal pool with lots of anemones and urchins.

But as I lower Helen, a hermit crab stretches out a massive front claw. I've heard that crabs fight a lot, and that it's not about how big the crab is, but about the size of the claw. I'm not leaving Helen here.

I leap to another rock that has a tidal pool filled with snails and mussels. It has hermit crabs and regular crabs like Helen, but their claws are smaller than hers. Helen could be boss here. I lower her in the water and let go.

Helen doesn't move. "It's okay. You're free," I whisper.

But Helen is frozen. Maybe she's dead! I push her with my finger. "It's not your home pool, but you'll be okay."

An engine blubbers in the distance. Fishers on a bright yellow fishing boat haul in a lobster trap. I hope the trap's empty. I look back at the pool. Helen has snuck away! "Helen?"

Snails inch across the rocks. Hermit crabs wave their pincers. Finally, a little crab scuttles sideways across the bottom of the pool, stopping to straighten her path every few scuttles. One, two, three, four, five legs. It's Helen, all right. A seagull caws and flies over, darkening the pool. Helen scurries under a rock.

"You'll be fine," I say. My voice ripples the surface of the water. "Goodbye. I'll be more careful about where I step."

A cool breeze blows. Goose bumps sprout on my arms. It will be suppertime soon. Time to get home. But when I stand and look around, I can't believe what I see.

Water.

All around me, closing in on my feet! When I wasn't looking, the tide came up high. I'm trapped. I'm not a strong swimmer. I can't get home without help.

A car rumbles by on the road. I wave my arms and jump. "Hey!" But the driver doesn't see me. The sea surges. Cold water pours over the tops of my boots. I *have* to get to higher ground where I can wait for the tide to go out again.

Another car putters along the road. Our blue Honda! It grinds up to the house. Mom and Rudy step out. Rudy's barbered head gleams. "Hey!" I shout. I wave my arms. "Hey!" Mom and Rudy don't hear me. I whistle through my diastema, the way Rachel taught me, but they only head up the crooked steps into

our crooked house and slam the door hard behind them. It has to be slammed hard because of the crookedness.

The windows light up as Mom and Rudy move through the house. First the kitchen lights, then the living-room lamps. The house looks cozy under the darkening sky. Mom will be calling for me. When I don't answer, she'll just think I'm outside playing, or maybe at Rachel's. She won't realize I'm stuck in the middle of the ocean. Stranded on a rock. Marooned.

She's probably putting out crackers, hummus and a glass of milk on the kitchen table. And Rudy's just sitting there, leafing through his stupid thesaurus, not realizing how lucky he is. My fingers itch to trace the swirls on the tablecloth. I imagine the blackberry-juice stain left over from when Rachel and Jerry came over for breakfast. That blackberry pie was the best pie I've ever eaten. It tasted like it was *alive*. The water swirling around my feet feels alive too. It breathes. In and out.

"Help!" I scream into the salty air. "Help!" I pour the water out of my boots, remove my wet socks. My feet are pale and puckered and freezing. I wring out my socks and tug them back on. I walk to the edge of the rock. The grip of the prickly barnacles keeps me from slipping. A little ways away, a large rock curves above the water like a whale's back. It's far, but I think I can make it. I jump over water, landing on barnacles, cutting my hands. Barnacles are both helpful and treacherous. I lick the blood from the cuts. It's salty. Like the ocean.

And then I cry. Salt water pours from my eyes. I watch as the rock I just abandoned sinks lower into the water, then—*blub*—goes completely under.

"Hey!" I scream in the direction of the farmhouse. A light goes on upstairs. Rudy is probably getting something from his room. Maybe he's getting his cozies on—that's what my family calls pajamas. My heart lurches. I want to be home. So badly.

The sun is low in the sky. The lobster boat is a tiny dot in the distance. At least Helen is probably fine. She may have only five legs, but she has gills so she can breathe. I wish I had gills.

I blow on my hands to warm them up. My rock is almost entirely underwater. I'm on a little bump thick with barnacles, a tiny, prickly stage. A seagull swoops low, right past me. I can hear her wings *whoosh* against the air. "Hey," I call. It's ridiculous. As if she could help me. Let me hang on to her leg and carry me to shore?

I see Wigglechin pawing at the farmhouse door. The door opens to let her in. It's my chance! "HELP!" I scream. Wigglechin vanishes into the house. The door closes behind her.

The water is still rising. I take a deep breath. And then I let out one enormous yell. It fills my head, gallops across the ocean, shakes the sky: *"HHHEEEELLPP MEEE!"*

Chapter Seven

A great wheezing noise fills the air, like a logging truck blowing its horn. It's followed by a high-pitched squeak. It's like the kitchen-cupboard door squawking on its hinges, only a thousand times louder.

The noise blares over and over. What *is* it?

Rumpley!

Rumpley is walking down the driveway. *Hee haw. Hee haw.* He's crossing the road!

"No! Rumpley! You'll get hurt!"

Rumpley is heading to the shore. At the water's edge he raises his heavy head and looks at me. *Hee haw!*

Rumpley raises his front foot.

"Don't go in the water! You'll drown yourself. It's rough and—"

Rumpley steps right into the sea.

"Careful!"

Rumpley never stumbles. He walks until he's up to his neck, then starts swimming! He comes closer and closer. Finally, he's right near me. I touch his nose. "You silly donkey!" Rumpley swings his head and touches his back with his muzzle. He snorts. He muzzles his back again.

"I'll try," I say. I grab hold of his short mane and swing a leg over. I lie low on his back, pressing against his furry warmth as he makes his way over the rocks toward shore. Up and down, I rock with each step, like ocean waves, until Rumpley steps slowly out of the water onto dry land. He keeps going.

When we're crossing the road, Jerry's truck comes barreling around the corner. Jerry hits the brakes, and he and Rachel stare as Rumpley carries me up the driveway, both of us dripping wet. Jerry jumps out to help me down, and Rachel runs to get Mom from the house. "Get a towel for Cyrus and a blanket for Rumpley," I hear Mom tell Rudy.

When I tell her what happened and how Rumpley saved me, she starts to cry.

"I had no idea," she says. "I was stirring the soup and you were out there, nearly dead!"

Rachel, today all in yellow, throws a blanket over Rumpley while Jerry checks his hooves. "Not a scratch or a nick," he says. "This donkey's strong as an ox. You've been looking after him well."

I head inside for a hot bath. When I'm at the door, Rachel calls to me. "The flag's fixed. We're raising it this evening. I hope you can come and watch."

So after I've thawed out in the bath and put on my cozies, Rudy and I cut through the hedge. Halfway in, I take a spoon from my pocket and dig a small hole. As we pat the dirt over Helen's leg, I recite the poem I wrote.

Here lies Helen's sixth leg.
If she was a pirate, she'd have a peg.
But she's a tough five-legged crab
Who crawls the sea, doing fab.

It was hard to find something that rhymes with *crab*. Rudy had to consult his ancient book.

Corny has mended the flag really well. The seams don't match up perfectly, but you can't tell unless you're really staring at it.

"It's going all the way to the top," Rachel says. "No more half-mast sadness. Thanks to you, Cyrus."

"*Me?*"

"You mended Rumpley's spirit," Jerry says. "I thought I'd never hear him bray again. Hector can rest in peace now."

He hands me the rope. Hand over hand, I pull until the flag reaches the very top of the pole. As the flag flaps in the evening wind, Rumpley starts to bray as if he knows. Then the chickens join in, clucking. And the cows start mooing. And Rachel and I whistle through our teeth. I guess that's the way we celebrate in the country.

Sara Cassidy has worked as a youth-hostel manager, a newspaper reporter and a tree planter in five Canadian provinces. Her poetry, fiction and articles have been widely published, and she has won a Gold National Magazine Award. She lives in Victoria, British Columbia, with her three children. For more information, visit www.saracassidywriter.com.

Also by SARA CASSIDY

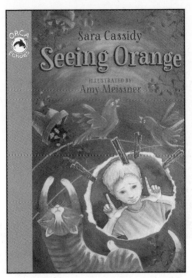

9781554699919 • $6.95 PB • Ages 7–9
9781554699964 (pdf) • 9781459803183 (epub)

LELAND'S ARTISTIC GIFTS HELP LEAD HIM TO FIND THE COURAGE HE NEEDS.

"Full of vivid descriptions and emotion, this book will attract a wide range of readers."
—*Library Media Connection*

ORCA BOOK PUBLISHERS
www.orcabook.com • 1-800-210-5277

READ THE FIRST CHAPTER OF
SARA CASSIDY'S' *SEEING ORANGE*

Chapter One

Pumpkin is stretched out asleep in my pajama drawer. Now my pajamas will have her golden-orange hairs all over them.

Mom is reading on the front steps, a mug of smelly tea by her knee. She calls it *herbal* tea. But I call it *horrible* tea.

My sister Liza is singing in the bathtub. It's some song about setting fire to the rain. Liza only takes baths so she can sing in the bathroom. She likes the echoes. She calls them *acoustics*.

Silas is building LEGO spaceships on the floor of our frog-green bedroom. Later, he'll head outside to throw a tennis ball against the wall. Once, his ball went through the open bathroom window while Liza was in there singing. *Splash!* Did Liza ever scream!

And me? I'm under the piano bench. I've draped a blanket over it to make a secret cave. It's getting pretty hot in here. Maybe I'll go lie on the floor in the narrow space between Mom's bed and the wall. I could pretend I'm a luger speeding down an ice track. That'll cool me down.

I like the laundry room best. It's a scrubbed place. The air smells like soap. I like the white walls and the soft towers of clean, folded laundry. The only problem is the dirty laundry piled on the cement floor. It's like a stinky sleeping beast. If I look too long, it starts to breathe.

This morning, I drew a picture of Mom's sweater on the clothesline. The crayon that matched it was called persimmon. Apricot was too light. It was hard to draw the sweater's wrinkles. But I did a good job with the right sleeve that hung down as if it was reaching for something.

The kitchen is the busy room in our house. It's where we talk and play Scrabble. Silas doesn't

usually sit for long. He wheels around and around the house on his Rollerblades. He only changes direction if he gets dizzy. "He'll damage the floors," visitors warn. Mom just shakes her head. "Having fun is more important than smooth floors," she says.

Some places in our house scare me. Like under the back porch. I only go there if we are playing hide-and-seek. I squat on top of the broken plant pots, hoping the pill bugs don't crawl over me. Old flower bouquets with brown petals and moldy stems rot in the dirt. Mom dumps vases out there when she can't get to the compost pile.

On school mornings, we jam up in our tiny front hallway. We cram our lunches into our schoolbags. Mom searches frantically for the car keys. Silas gulps down the last of his bowl of cereal. Liza pulls everything off the coat hooks to look for her favorite hoodie.

Move out of the way!

Where's my other shoe?

That's MY lunch.

Mom calls it the Hurry Flurry. These days, I don't like the Hurry Flurry. Because I don't want to go to school. My grade two teacher is Mr. Carling. No matter what I do, he's always mad at me.